Boarder Boys

Boarder Boys

Book One: Mystery of the Giant

Brenda Sweeney

iUniverse, Inc.
Bloomington

Boarder Boys
Book One: Mystery of the Giant

iUniverse books may be ordered through booksellers or by contacting:

iUniverse
1663 Liberty Drive
Bloomington, IN 47403
www.iuniverse.com
1-800-Authors (1-800-288-4677)

ISBN: 978-1-4759-6599-5 (sc)
ISBN: 978-1-4759-6601-5 (ebk)

Library of Congress Control Number: 2012923334

Printed in the United States of America

iUniverse rev. date: 02/13/2013

For Jake and Rachel Sweeney

Chapter 1

"I can't do it!" Jake yelled over the whir of the helicopter. Sweat dripped off his brow, in spite of the cold. He couldn't seem to get his breathing under control. How could he be panting like he'd just run a marathon, when he'd been sitting in the helicopter for half an hour. He glanced at his friend. Nothing ever seemed to shake Patrick up. Patrick was the calmest, coolest guy Jake had ever met. Of course, Patrick had done this before. *I'll be calm the next time . . . if I live through this.* Jake shook his head and leaned closer so Patrick could hear him complain. "I don't know how you talked me into this! I could be using a lift in Vail, like a normal person. Next time remind me that I don't want to listen to you."

"You can do it!" Patrick yelled back.

"That's easy for you to say!" Patrick had been skiing and snowboarding since he was three years old and competing since he was twelve. Jake was a beginner by comparison.

"Not that different from the back bowls," Patrick insisted. When Jake pointed at the distance between the copter and the snow, Patrick shrugged.

"Just close your eyes and jump!" Patrick gave Jake a friendly push out the helicopter door, and followed him almost immediately.

Jakes 6'2", lean body, landed in waist deep powder. His short black hair was hidden under his black helmet. Patrick's shorter muscular frame landed near Jake. His short blonde curls were peeking out from under his orange helmet. With a yell, Jake followed Patrick. As they cut their way down the mountain, Jake decided Patrick was right. There was nothing in the world better than cutting fresh tracks in the snow. *Free like a bird. Just like Patrick had said. What an incredible feeling!*

"Whoooh!" yelled Jake as he cut back and forth across the powder. "You are right. This is incredible!" Jake relaxed as he focused on the powder in front of him. He was stoked to be in such a beautiful place. The contrast between the bright blue sky and the crisp white snow was striking. And the silence was very peaceful. The only sound was the sound of the two snowboards cutting through the snow with ease. *I wonder if heaven is this beautiful.* Jake came back sharply from his thoughts and caught his breath as he saw Patrick up ahead. Patrick was rapidly approaching a large pile of rocks and he didn't seem to be trying to avoid it. Jake slowed and watched as his best friend flew up over the snowy side of the rocks. Patrick went airborne for what seemed like hours to Jake.

Jake watched Patrick grab his board, flip, twist and stomp the landing. *That must be the new trick that he told me about.* Jake laughed and shook his head at his friend showing off. Jake knew Patrick was good, but he didn't know he was that good. Jake had no intention of doing any tricks. His focus was just on getting down the mountain safely. Jake had promised his mom he wouldn't do anything crazy, when he had begged her for permission to go heli-boarding.

"Yeah! This is sick!" yelled Patrick. "Catch air on the next rocks Jake!"

Jake was gaining quite a bit of speed as he approached the next rock outcropping. *Can I do it? Can I fly through the air like Patrick?* He was confident in his snowboarding abilities, but this was something totally different. He knew that his helmet could only do so much to protect his head. *I'm not going to fall on the rocks, am I?* Suddenly Jake knew he could do it. He had jumped over smaller rocks many times. He had done plenty of jumps, flips, and twists in the jump park. He knew what to do. Jake just had to see himself making it over the rocks and he would do just fine. "Watch this," he yelled to Patrick.

Patrick stopped and watched his friend go straight for the rocks. His mouth opened with surprise, as Jake flew up over the rocks, did a simple toe grab, and landed easily. Both boys cheered with excitement. This was paradise.

Patrick and Jake would both snowboard everyday if they could. Patrick came pretty close to it. He had practically grown up in the mountains. He saved his money every year so he could buy a season pass to ski in the mountains of Colorado. Whenever possible, Patrick rushed from school straight to the slopes to get a run in before the lifts closed.

Jake, on the other hand, had only lived in Vail for three years. His family moved from Highlands Ranch, CO, when his parents decided to escape from the high-tech industry and start their own ski and bike shop. Jake was in 7th grade when they moved. He wasn't excited about the move at first, but he had always loved the mountains and liked the idea of being able to ski every weekend in the winter. Jake was a 16 year old sophomore in high school now, and was very involved in extracurricular activities. He played on the football, basketball, and baseball teams. He was also very active with the youth group at church. Therefore, he didn't get to the slopes very often during the week. But he rarely missed a weekend of snowboarding.

The boys continued to carve the mountain at lightening speed. They zipped back and forth and darted around trees. There were a lot of tall, beautiful pine trees on this side of the mountain. Every now and then the pine trees were divided by a group of Aspen swaying in the breeze. The fresh powder was spraying up above the boys' heads. Whenever possible, they went off a jump and caught air.

After awhile, the boys decided to take a break and eat lunch. "I see some big, flat rocks up ahead," said Jake. "This looks like a good spot for lunch."

"What did you pack for lunch?" asked Patrick.

"A ham sandwich and cookies, along with the apple and carrots that my mom tried to sneak in my lunch bag when I wasn't looking," replied Jake. "What about you? Did you bring anything I might want to trade you for?"

"I pretty much brought the same as you. And I also managed to snag a couple of my mom's brownies," Patrick said with a smile. "I thought that they might interest you."

"Interest me?" cried Jake. "Your mom's brownies are my favorite dessert in the world! I'll trade you my whole lunch for one of your mom's brownies!"

"How about you just give me one of your cookies and I will give you one of my brownies," replied Patrick.

"That's a deal dude," Jake said as he pulled his food out of his backpack.

It didn't take long for the boys to finish their lunch. They had really worked up an appetite snowboarding. After lunch, Jake and Patrick both decided to lie back on the rocks and rest for a little while. While they were lying there with their eyes closed, they heard a loud noise that made them both sit up and look around.

"What was that?" asked Jake.

"I don't know," replied Patrick. "I don't think it was an animal. But yet, it didn't really sound like a person either."

"Let's check it out," said Jake. "I think the sound came from over there." Jake pointed to the edge of a heavily wooded area and began to walk over to it. Patrick followed closely. As they got to the edge of the trees, they saw some tracks in the snow.

"That's strange," said Patrick as he looked around for more tracks. "This looks like someone dragged something pretty heavy through here. I've been up here many times without ever seeing another human being. What could they possibly be dragging?"

"And why would they drag it up hill?" asked Jake. "It looks like it was heavy. That would be a lot of work to drag something that heavy uphill. Where could they possibly be going with it?"

"I don't know," responded Patrick. "But we are about to find out. Let's follow the tracks."

The boys quickly ran back to get their backpacks and snowboards. What they didn't realize was that they weren't alone.

Chapter 2

Jake and Patrick walked along the narrow trail, carrying their snowboards. The trees were big and close together. The trail wound back and forth around the trees. The trail had a lot of switchbacks because the ground was so steep.

"It's starting to get dark under these trees," commented Jake. "It must be clouding up. I didn't think the clouds were supposed to move in until later tonight."

"I hope it holds off long enough for us to hike this trail and then snowboard back down to the car," said Patrick with a frown. "I've been caught up in a snow storm up here before, and I really don't care to do it again any time soon."

"We especially don't want to get caught up here today! We really need to get back for Aaron's birthday celebration. It is a surprise party and Rachel said we have to get there before Aaron arrives. She and Maddie are working hard on setting up the party at our house. She won't let me hear the end of it if we are late."

"Speaking of your little sister . . . I heard that Rachel took first place in the Boardercross competition last weekend. That's incredible!" said Patrick.

"I am always amazed at how well she does, with so little practice time on her snowboard. Her basketball team practices almost every day this time of year. Friday night she was the high scorer in her basketball game, and then Saturday she won her Boardercross competition. The girl is a gifted athlete," said Jake with admiration

The boys continued to hike in silence for a while. Suddenly the trail opened up to a large clearing. Jake and Patrick stopped to look around. The view was spectacular. They could see out over the valley and several other mountaintops. They could see a nearby ski resort. The skiers looked like small dots zigzagging back and forth as they zoomed down the runs. The lifts looked like distant telephone poles and wires. Over on the next peak, the boys could see a herd of big horn sheep as they grazed on the side of the mountain.

"Wow, what a view!" exclaimed Patrick. "We can see for miles!"

"The view is awesome," agreed Jake. "Wow, look at the dark clouds forming over there! It looks like a serious snow storm is heading our way. We need to get down the mountain and fast!"

"You're right, those clouds look pretty bad. I say we forget this trail and get out of here while we can still see to find our way down the mountain," said Patrick with a serious look on his face.

"I'm with you on that dude," agreed Jake. "But let's come back here tomorrow to check out this trail. I really want to know where it leads to, and what is being pulled up the mountain. It just seems pretty odd to me."

"That's a deal," said Patrick

"Whoa!" yelled Jake as his foot slipped out from under him. He fell onto his back and started to slide down the side of the mountain. Jake tried to reach out and grab a tree as he began to slide, but instead of a tree, he got Patrick's leg. So they both went sliding rapidly down the mountain. As they slid through the clearing, Jake realized that they were gaining speed. Somehow they needed to slow down before they made it all of the way to the next group of trees. He really didn't feel like breaking a bone on a tree trunk. *At least we have our helmets on*, he thought as his mind raced trying to come up with an idea on how to slow them both down. Just then two Golden Retrievers came from out of nowhere. One grabbed Jake's arm and the other grabbed Patrick's leg. The dogs tried to plant their feet and stop the boys' slide. The dogs slid with them for a few feet, before they slowed down enough that the boys were able to stop themselves. Once their mission was completed, the dogs let go of the boys and licked their faces. Jake and Patrick began to laugh as they pet the friendly dogs.

"Thanks doggie," said Jake. "Patrick, did you see where these guys came from?"

"No! I was surprised when this guy grabbed my leg. I'm not going to complain though. They probably saved us from a serious injury."

While Jake and Patrick were still petting and talking to the dogs, a boy suddenly appeared at the edge of the clearing. The boy looked like he was about 14 years old. He was wearing a tattered black shirt under a worn ski jacket, and faded jeans with several holes in them. The jeans were a little too big for him, so he had a belt cinched around his waist to hold them up. The boy had black, shoulder length hair. "Carmel, Wylie, come here girls. Let's go!" the boy said with a stern voice. When the dogs didn't respond immediately, the boy almost barked, "Come!" The dogs responded to the command and ran to him. As soon as the dogs were at his side, the boy began to walk back into the woods.

"Wait!" yelled Patrick. "We just want to thank you." But the boy was already out of their sight. Patrick and Jake tried to run up the hill to where they last saw the younger boy. But it was a steep slope, and they were a little shaken up from the fall, so their legs weren't moving very quickly. The boys both felt like they were trying to run in waist deep water. They tried so hard to move quickly, but they might as well be crawling. By the time they got to the edge of the clearing, the mysterious boy and his dogs were nowhere to be seen. They had vanished as mysteriously as they had appeared.

"Nobody would believe this story, if I didn't have you as a witness," stated Patrick.

"Isn't that the truth? I am a witness, but yet I'm not sure if I even believe it," replied Jake. "There is no denying the fact that the dogs stopped our fall. I even have the holes in my jacket to prove it. This whole day is starting to seem pretty strange—an unexplained trail and a mysterious boy with two dogs come from out of nowhere and then vanish just as quickly. Where do you think the boy and his dogs could have gone?"

"I don't know," said Patrick. "I've been up here many times, and have never seen anything but rocks, trees, and snow. I say we come back here tomorrow and do a little exploring. I'd like to know what that boy was doing up here and why he was conveniently in a position to help us out of a jam."

"Keep in mind that he didn't have to help us. By helping us, he gave up his cover, so to speak. So he can't be all bad."

"I still have a feeling that he is up to no good. I can't explain it. It is just a feeling. Okay, let's get out of here before the snow storm hits," Patrick said as he dropped his snowboard down on the snow.

Once again, they thought they were alone . . . . but they weren't.

Chapter 3

"Wow! You guys really did a good job decorating the place!" exclaimed Jake. "Maybe you should start a party business. This is obviously something that you both are very good at."

"Flattery will get you everywhere," responded Rachel with a smile. "I'm glad you like the way it turned out. We worked hard on this. It took us hours."

"I'll bet," said Patrick. "Whose idea was it to hang a net full of balloons on the ceiling? That should really surprise him."

"That was my idea," said Maddie. "It's possible that somehow Aaron heard about the party. If that is the case, he won't be too surprised when he walks in and sees everyone. But he will be surprised when 200 balloons fall on his head!"

"Two hundred balloons!" exclaimed Jake. "No wonder it took you hours. You ladies are full of more hot air than I ever imagined."

"Very funny," responded Rachel as she pretended to hit Jake's arm. "We have actually been blowing the balloons up a few at a time over the last week. We didn't want to pass out from blowing them up at once."

Just then, the doorbell rang. The first guests had arrived. Over the next 30 minutes, about 25 more people arrived for the party. They followed instructions and parked their cars at the school and walked the block to Jake and Rachel's house. Some of the guests lived close enough that they were able to walk from home to the party. Finally, it was time for everyone to hide. They all went into the family room so they couldn't be seen from the front entry. At first, they waited quietly. But as the minutes passed and there was no sign of Aaron, they began to whisper. After a while, the whispers became a low murmur, the murmur eventually grew to a loud roar. They almost forgot that they were waiting for Aaron, when the doorbell rang.

"Shhhhh!" commanded Rachel in a loud whisper. The group huddled together so that they couldn't be seen from around the corner. Rachel went to the door and opened it with a smile. "Hi, Aaron, are you looking for Jake?"

"No, my mom asked me to stop by to pick up some stuff that your mom said she could borrow. I don't even know what it is. I only know that I am supposed to get it and bring it home for her," responded Aaron appearing to have no idea that 30 of his friends were all frozen in silence on the other side of the stairs.

"Hmmmm, my mom didn't mention anything about having stuff for your mom. Come on in and I will check with her. She is in the kitchen." Aaron stepped into the house and closed the door. He followed Rachel across the wood floor in the entryway. Rachel stepped down into the family room and rounded the corner. Aaron was about to step down when the balloons came down on his head, and he heard a loud "Surprise!" Everyone came out from around the corner. They all laughed at the shocked look on Aaron's face.

"Wow, I had absolutely no idea! I can't believe you were able to pull this off without me hearing about it," Aaron said with amazement. "I didn't even see any cars outside. Where did everyone park?"

"Most of us parked up at the school so you wouldn't notice the cars and blow the surprise," replied Patrick. "Happy Birthday, Aaron!"

Everyone began talking again. The music was turned up and they began to dive into the food. Rachel and Maddie made twice as much food as they needed, including three desserts in addition to the birthday cake. The desserts seemed to be quite a hit.

"Where is Mom?" asked Jake. "I know she would never let us have a party without her chaperoning."

"She's working out in the basement. She promised to stay out of our way. She just wants to be here in case there is a problem. Mom said she could use a good workout, anyway. Dad just installed her punching bag this morning, and she couldn't wait to try it out."

"Oh great! I can't wait to try it out myself," Jake replied. "I'm going to go downstairs and say 'Hi.'"

But before Jake started down the stairs, he overheard his classmate, Stephen, talking about being robbed. Jake hurried over to the group and joined in their conversation.

"Stephen, I thought I heard you say that you were robbed," said Jake with genuine concern. "Is that right? What happened? What did they take?"

"Whoa, dude, slow down with the questions and give me a chance to tell you what happened. Yes, you heard right. I was robbed. But not like you would think. No one broke into our home or anything like that. Today while we were skiing, someone smashed the window of my car. They must have used a baseball bat or something similar. Glass was all over the inside of the car. They went into the glove box and took all four of our wallets. They took my case of CDs, our sunglasses, my cell phone, and even our cooler with our lunch in it," said Stephen, looking pretty upset about the ordeal. "How low is that? We discovered it when we went back to the car to get our lunch. What a shock to see splintered glass all over the car. It was almost like they knew we had wallets in the glove box."

"And that's not all. While we were waiting for the police to come, we walked around the parking lot looking to see if they had taken the money and tossed the wallets," added Stephen. "It would be nice to not have to replace our driver's licenses, membership cards, and all of that stuff. As we began to look around, we noticed other small piles of glass—several other small piles of glass. We apparently were not the only victims in the parking lot today. There had been others today as well as other days. It really looked like this had been going on for quite a while. And whoever is doing it is getting quite experienced," Stephen said as he kicked the floor.

"You won't believe where they were parked," Patrick said to Jake

"Where?" asked Jake.

"Just two rows over from our car," answered Patrick. "And I didn't even notice any broken windows or glass on the ground, when we were there."

"Neither did I, until I had a broken window," replied Stephen. "It's the kind of thing that you just don't notice, unless you are looking for it. The police officer said that this has been happening a lot lately. He thinks that someone living in the area is doing it. Whoever it is even tries to use the bankcards they find in the stolen wallets. Of course they can't figure out the code, so the machine takes the card after a few tries. They seem to cover the ATM camera when they try to use the stolen card, so there is no video to help identify the criminal."

"What do you think makes them choose one car over another?" asked Patrick. "Our car was parked there almost all day, and they didn't touch it."

"Maybe it depends on activity level in the parking lot at the time you park," replied Jake. "Or maybe Stephen's car was a good hit because it could have as many as four wallets in it, while ours wouldn't have had more than two."

"I don't know," replied Stephen. "But I do know that I won't leave any valuables in my car again. And it will be awhile before I park in that lot again, too."

The boys then began discussing more interesting things, like which teams they thought would make it to the Super Bowl. After awhile, Aaron opened his gifts. Several people brought gag gifts and this really got everyone laughing. Soon after the gifts were opened, people started to leave. Once everyone was gone, Jake, Rachel, and Patrick cleaned up. When they were finished cleaning, Patrick got ready to leave.

"Hey, do you want to stay and watch a movie?" asked Rachel. "I rented one that looks pretty good. And I promise it is an action movie, not a romance."

"Thanks, but I can't," replied Patrick. "I need to get home and do some reading and planning. I'm teaching a 2nd grade Sunday school class tomorrow morning, and I haven't planned my lesson yet. My mom usually teaches this class, but tomorrow she is singing in church, and she asked me to be her substitute. I have helped out with little kids before, but have never had to actually teach a lesson. I'm a little nervous!"

"Do you want to snowboard after church?" asked Jake.

"You bet I do. I'll put my stuff in the car and we can head out straight from church."

"Sounds like a plan. I will see you in the morning," said Jake as he opened the front door for Patrick. The crisp night air felt so good that Jake walked out on the front porch with Patrick. "What a beautiful night!" Jake exclaimed. "The cool air really feels good. And look at all of those stars! I hope this is a sign that tomorrow will be a nice day."

"They are predicting snow later tonight, a sunny day tomorrow and more snow tomorrow night. It sounds like we will need some sunscreen tomorrow. A perfect day to snowboard," said Patrick as he got into his car. "Oh, yeah, do you still want to go check out the area where the mysterious boy was today?"

"Yes, I do want to check it out. Let's take the snowmobiles part way, so we can get over there quicker," suggested Jake.

"You got it! Have a good night," said Patrick as he closed the door to his four-wheel drive pick-up truck. It was really his dad's truck. But Patrick drove it so much, everyone thought it was his. His parents didn't believe in giving a car to a 16 year old. They believed that teenagers need to work hard and save their money, so they could buy their own car. Patrick worked during the summer, but during the school year he didn't have time to work, because school and snowboarding took up so much of his time. Most of the money he earned paid for gas or snowboarding equipment, so he wasn't saving for a car very quickly. As long as Patrick's parents know where he is going and who he is with, they let him take the truck whenever he wants it. This works out well for both Patrick and Jake, since Patrick has a pickup truck with plenty of room for their snowboards.

Jake stood in the front yard looking at the stars, as Patrick drove away, down the steeply sloped driveway. He was always amazed at how many stars God had put in the galaxy. Scientists estimate that there are 200 to 400 billion stars in the Milky Way Galaxy, and there are up to 500 galaxies. The numbers were hard for Jake to get his head around. He could see some clouds moving in, so Patrick's weather report sounded like it was correct. Jake started to think about the boy in the woods. It was just too strange the way he came from out of nowhere. And how the boy was probably the only other human on that side of the mountain today, and he just happened to be in the same area as the boys. *It was a little too coincidental. And that trail . . . what was that all about?* As Jake slept that night, he dreamed about sliding down a mountain and being saved by a mysterious boy and his dog.

Chapter 4

Sunday morning Patrick walked into the 2nd grade Sunday school classroom and found a surprise waiting for him. Rachel was there playing with the one child who had shown up early.

"What are you doing here?" asked Patrick with a surprised smile.

"I thought you could use a little help," replied Rachel as she walked across the room. "Last night you didn't sound too experienced with 2nd graders. I taught 2nd grade Vacation Bible School last summer, so I thought I could be a little help to you."

"Wow, you are a life saver!" exclaimed Patrick. "I didn't realize I was so nervous about this, until I got into the car to drive over here. Thanks, I really owe you for this."

"No worries."

As the children began to arrive, Rachel kept them entertained while Patrick checked them in. The kids all seemed to enjoy Patrick's lesson. Their favorite part was clearly Bible Tic-Tac-Toe. After the children left, Jake showed up at the door.

"Perfect timing!" said Rachel, sarcastically. "Where were you when 20 second graders were running around here like this was a playground? We could have used your help."

"Sorry I couldn't help. I had band practice down the hall. We are playing for the high school youth group in a couple of weeks, and we really haven't played together much."

"Nice excuse. We'll let you slide on it this time," said Rachel as she jabbed Jake with her elbow.

"Let's clean up and get out of here," said Patrick. "The slopes are calling our names."

The three quickly cleaned up the classroom and headed out. Jake loaded his ski gear into Patrick's truck. Patrick noticed that Rachel didn't have her gear with her. "Rachel, aren't you going with us this afternoon?"

"No thanks. I'm going to have to pass on snowboarding. I've got to get a lot of things done today. But I will definitely snowboard with you guys next weekend."

"OK. But you are going to miss a good time. They got over 6 inches of fresh powder last night. And there isn't a cloud in the sky. Jake and I are going to take the snowmobiles out for a spin before we snowboard."

"Oh wow! I haven't been on a snowmobile all winter! I would love to go with you guys. But I promised Mom I would do a few things with her today. Then, of course, there is the homework that I have put off all weekend. Monday morning is coming quickly, and I am running out of time to get it done."

"No problem. We will put you on the list of attendees for next weekend," said Patrick.

Patrick stopped the truck to let Rachel out in front of her house. She walked to the front door, stopped to wave, and yelled to the boys to not have too much fun without her.

Patrick headed towards Jake's parents' ski shop, where they store their snowmobiles. They have a small shed in the back that is the perfect size for the trailer. Patrick backed up to the shed. Jake hopped out of the truck, opened the shed doors, and hooked the trailer to the truck. They were both pros at this. They had been hooking the trailer to a hitch years before they were even old enough to drive. Once the trailer was safely attached to the truck, they drove to the parking lot where they had parked the day before. This time they looked around the parking lot carefully to see if there was anyone watching them getting out of their car. Once they felt sure that there wasn't anyone around, they put their CD case in the glove compartment and locked it. Just to be on the safe side, they put their wallets in the pockets of their ski jackets. They didn't want to have to deal with a broken window and missing wallets.

The boys carefully took the snowmobiles off of the trailer, loaded their snowboards on the back, and put on their backpacks. Their backpacks were full of backcountry safety gear. They never snowboarded without their helmets, GPS, avalanche beacons, probes and shovels. Their parents made sure they were both trained in backcountry navigation, and taught them to use maps and a GPS at a very young age. Their parents also made them take several avalanche safety courses, before ever letting them snowboard in the backcountry. Patrick used his avalanche safety gear once, but Jake had only used his for practice.

They didn't talk much while they were preparing for their journey. They were both wondering whether or not anyone was watching them from behind the trees.

"So Patrick, how do you think we should approach that area? If we just ride straight there, the noise of the snowmobiles will tip off anyone up there. They will have plenty of time to pack up and move out before we ever get a chance to find them."

"I have already thought about that," said Patrick. "I think we should ride up far to the east of the area and go up almost to the top of the mountain. There are always a lot of snowmobiles in that area where the ground levels out, so our noise shouldn't tip anyone off. We can park the snowmobiles and hike across the mountain and down to the area on our snowshoes. That way no one will hear us unless they are listening for us."

"The only down side is if we need a quick getaway, we will be running uphill, and pretty far, to get to the snowmobiles."

"What or who do you think we will be running from?" asked Patrick. "We are just going to silently check the area out and see what is there. We aren't looking for any trouble. If we see anything, we will leave immediately and head right for the nearest police station. I promise."

"Yeah, I have heard that promise before," said Jake skeptically. "OK, I'll go along with your plan. But I want you to understand that as soon as we see what is going on, we are out of there. Got it?"

"Got it!"

Chapter 5

The boys started their snowmobiles and headed up the mountain. They had to go pretty far up the mountain, but it didn't take too long on snowmobiles. It was a beautiful clear day. The sun light danced on the snow and would have blinded anyone who didn't have good sunglasses on. There wasn't a single cloud in the beautiful blue sky. Jake looked up at the tall green pine trees and thought that the view looked like a postcard. He made a mental note to bring his camera with him next time, so he could capture the beauty of the slope and send it to his relatives in Florida. Jake and his cousins had a constant debate about who lived in the most beautiful place. He felt sure that a picture of this would end the debate. No one in their right mind could deny that this was the most beautiful sight they had ever seen.

Jake and Patrick followed their plan of heading to the east of the area they wanted to inspect, where there were several other snowmobiles in the area, so the noise of their snowmobiles wouldn't alert anyone to their presence. They tried to go up higher on the mountain than the area they were in yesterday, so that they could walk down and across the mountain quietly. There were quite a few trees along the way, so they couldn't go full speed. They had to really pay attention to their steering in order to avoid a collision. They both knew that in a battle between a tree and snowmobile, the tree would win every time.

When they thought that they had gone high enough, Patrick and Jake stopped and parked their snowmobiles in some thick trees. They didn't want anyone to notice that the snowmobiles were there. Of course there wasn't a lot they could do about the tracks in the fresh snow. They tried to smooth out the tracks close to the snowmobiles, but it wasn't very effective.

Jake and Patrick put on their snowshoes, grabbed their backpacks full of backcountry equipment, and headed toward the spot where they saw tracks the day before. As they got close to the spot, the boys decided to walk in the trees as much as possible so that they wouldn't be noticed. *This is really making me nervous. I don't know why I agreed to an uphill emergency getaway plan!* The farther they went, the more nervous Jake became.

They hiked for quite awhile. So long, in fact, that Jake began to think that they had misjudged the location of the tracks. "You know, Patrick, maybe walking in the trees threw us off a little bit. I think we should have come to the trail by now."

"Don't give up hope just yet," replied Patrick. "I think we will find the path in just a few minutes. According to my GPS, we will intersect with the path a little farther west than yesterday. That is why the area doesn't look too familiar. I thought it would be a little safer to approach the trail from a different angle today."

"Wow, if you are worried about safety, then I really should be worried!" exclaimed Jake in a soft voice. He didn't want his voice to carry too far and alert anyone of their presence. Patrick was always a little more wild and daring than Jake. Safety wasn't usually at the top of his list of concerns. Jake was a little relieved that he wasn't the only one concerned about what or who they might run across. But at the same time, he couldn't help but think that maybe this wasn't such a good idea after all.

"There are the tracks! You were right Patrick! You really do know how to use that GPS!"

"Thanks. I have had a little practice." Patrick replied with a laugh. Jake knew that Patrick had an uncanny sense of direction. He didn't really understand how it worked. Patrick just said that he learned a long time ago to trust his instincts, and amazingly, his instincts had never let him down. He had even helped hunt for a man who was buried in an avalanche once. Between Patrick's instincts and a Golden Retriever who was trained for avalanche rescue, they were able to save the man who was buried. That was not an adventure that Patrick wanted to repeat any time soon. It took the rescuers almost 15 minutes to find the man, and they had really started to think that it might be too late. Generally people could survive about 15 minutes under snow, but to survive longer than that they would have to have dug a hole around their face, to give them additional air. The man's son had followed Patrick around in tears as they were searching the massive pile of snow for a sign. Patrick felt like the snow looked a little different in one spot, and really checked that area carefully. And fortunately the man's jacket had a built in avalanche beacon reflector. Patrick scanned the area and was able to detect the man with his beacon. There was a picture of the man's son hugging Patrick on the front page of the local paper the next day. Patrick was considered a hero for quite a while.

Jake and Patrick began to follow the trail. They were sure it was the same type of track as the one they saw yesterday, but it had to be fresh because the snow during the night would have covered yesterday's tracks. The track was smooth and wide and looked as if someone had been dragging something very heavy, and for quite a long way. Whoever was responsible for making this track must be very strong and probably pretty big. Jake and Patrick were both keenly aware of that.

The boys hiked a lot farther than they had anticipated. Patrick was the leader. Jake's head was spinning as he checked the sides and behind them. He knew that the element of surprise was a tough one to beat, and Jake wanted it on their side. Jake noticed that Patrick was also cautiously checking all around them. Jake knew it really bothered Patrick that the boy and his dogs appeared to come from out of nowhere yesterday. Usually he was much more observant and knew when someone was nearby. Patrick was doing everything he could to make sure the boy couldn't surprise them again.

"Patrick, look!" Jake called in a harsh whisper. Off to the left about 200 yards off the trail was a tent. As the boys looked more closely, they could see that the tracks they were following continued to head straight for a short distance and then turned left and headed to the campsite.

"Let's walk down to the tent and check it out," whispered Jake. "But let's stay off of the trail. I think it would be better if we walk down toward it through the trees."

"Good idea," replied Patrick. "Hey, wait. I thought you were worried about running into someone who is less than happy to see us? Have you changed your mind?"

"No. I'm still concerned. But I am also extremely curious as to who they are, and what they are doing here. This camp looks like it has been here for a long time. My guess is that these aren't campers. I think they live here and are probably up to no good. Are you coming?"

"Right behind you, boss," said Patrick with a smile, as he hurried up behind Jake. The boys slowly walked down toward the tent. Now their eyes were darting around very quickly as they watched for unfriendly company. This time Patrick was the one checking behind them. As they got closer to the tent, they could see that it was very worn and had holes in it. Near the tent was what looked like a homemade tent, made up of a few old tarps. The tarps also had holes in them, but most of the holes had been covered with duct tape. When they got within a few feet of the tent, they stopped and stood quietly for a few minutes. They were listening for any signs of life. They heard nothing, so after a while, Jake and Patrick walked cautiously up to the tent. They were able to peer in through the holes on the side. The tent appeared to be inhabited by two people. They could see two sleeping bags and two bumps that looked like they were being used as pillows. Jake stepped back and looked around. There was a thin rope tied between two trees that looked like it was being used as a clothesline. There were two worn towels hanging from the clothesline. The towels were so thin that you could almost see through them. There was a small fire ring not far from the tent, and it appeared to still be smoldering. This made Jake very angry because so many fires in Colorado are started from a smoldering fire that campers have left unattended. Snow on the ground does not guarantee that an accidental fire won't start. It also gave Jake the creeps because it made him think that whoever was living there hadn't been gone for long and therefore probably wasn't too far away. Jake turned to point this out to Patrick, but Patrick wasn't there. He had walked over to the tarps. The tarps were hung over ropes that were strung between trees. They appeared to be held together by duct tape and a couple of clothespins.

"Jake, come here!" shouted Patrick, forgetting to keep his voice down.

"Shhh, I'm coming," replied Jake. Jake walked over to Patrick, and they both stood there looking into the makeshift tent. On the ground under the tarps, the boys saw several large piles of stuff. As their eyes focused on the mounds, they both realized that it was a collection of expensive items. They saw countless radios, CD Players, CD cases, cell phones, jewelry, wallets, purses, sunglasses, and hubcaps. The guys couldn't believe what they were looking at. They just stood there staring at the hoard for what seemed like a long time, neither one of them speaking. They were both wondering whom this belonged to, and what it was doing under a tarp in the middle of the forest.

Jake was the first to break the silence. "Hey, look at the green wallet with the snowboard on it! That looks like Stephen's!" Jake was pointing to the wallet that was thrown on top of a heap of wallets. At this point, Jake forgot about being quiet. And they both forgot about keeping an eye out for surprise attackers.

Jake reached into the tent to grab the wallet that looked like Stephen's. As he turned to show it to Patrick, someone grabbed Jake and lifted him off of the ground by his collar. Jake was shocked because he hadn't heard anyone walk up. He was also scared because this guy was so big, and so angry. Jake dropped the wallet and threw his hands up in the air.

"What are you doing?" bellowed a man, who looked to Jake, a lot like Goliath, in a David and Goliath movie he had seen in Sunday school, when he was younger. The man had to be at least 6 feet 10 inches tall, and had to weigh at least 300 pounds. The man was unshaven, his clothes were such a mess that it looked like he had slept in them for days. He had a long, black, scraggly ponytail with streaks of gray in it. His face looked like he was snarling at the boys, and he seemed to be missing a few teeth. The teeth he still had were gray and black. The man had a long scar that went all the way across one side of his face.

Patrick had been looking at crowbars and baseball bats at the side of the tent and didn't see the man approach them. Someone had snuck up on the boys for the second time this weekend. And both boys were so shocked by the sudden appearance of the Giant, that neither one of them could think of a thing to say.

"I'll teach you boys about sneaking around other people's property!" bellowed the big man in a deep, loud voice. The man raised his hand as if he was going to slap Jake. Luckily instinct kicked in and Jake jerked himself out of the man's grasp. The gigantic man started to grab Jake's arm, when suddenly, the mysterious boy and his two dogs appeared again. The boy ran up to the man and got between him and Jake. The two dogs followed the boy, so now all three of them were between the Giant and Jake. Jake marveled at how brave the boy was, and briefly wondered why the boy was risking his own life to help a stranger. But he did not have time to linger on such thoughts. Jake knew that if he was going to get away, he had to take off now. And he also knew that he had to run faster than he had ever run in his life, and he had to do it in snowshoes. This man had very long legs and could easily overtake the boys on a sprint. But if Jake and Patrick could put some distance between them and the Giant, they might have a chance to escape unharmed.

Jake yelled, "Come on!" and he and Patrick began running like their life depended on it. That was because they truly thought that it did.

"I'm right behind you!" yelled Patrick. "Move it!"

Luckily the boys were both in very good shape. Jake and Patrick had both run a few 10k snowshoe races with their mothers, so they were pretty experienced with moving fast in snowshoes and were fortunate enough to have snowshoes that were made for racing. Speed is all that mattered right now. And that included not falling. If one of them fell, there is no way they could recover and get moving, before the Giant could descend upon them. Jake and Patrick were both very capable of running the two miles from the camp to their snowmobiles. The Giant had long legs, but he didn't look like he was in very good shape. And without snowshoes, he should be slow. If they could get some distance between them, there was no way he could catch up with them. Patrick was always a little faster than Jake. He took the lead and ran into the trees so it would be harder for the Giant to follow them. Jake looked back for a split second, before he ducked into the trees behind Patrick. He saw the man push the boy out of the way, and then start to run after them.

Jake and Patrick ran the entire two miles back to their snowmobiles without saying a word. One reason was because if the man couldn't see them or hear them, it would be harder for him to catch them. The other, probably more important reason, was they needed every bit of their oxygen for energy to run. Jake and Patrick were both breathing so hard that they thought their lungs would explode. They had never run in snowshoes this fast in their lives. Their mothers would have been proud of their speed.

As the boys approached the clump of trees where they had hidden their snowmobiles, Jake noticed quite a few footprints around the area, but he didn't have time to mention it to Patrick. They had to get out of there. NOW!

The boys were both relieved to know that they could ride on the snowmobiles now and give their lungs and legs a rest. They each tied their snowshoes down, jumped on their snowmobiles and took off instantly. They didn't go down the same path they had come up earlier that day. Jake thought it was best to take a different way down and was happy to see that Patrick must have been thinking the same thing, as he lead Jake down a new path.

The boys drove most of the way down the mountain before they stopped to talk about what just happened. They parked in a quiet, wooded area, where they couldn't be seen.

"Let's just get to the truck and get out of here," said Jake.

"Relax," replied Patrick. "Even if that guy could run fast, he didn't have any transportation. Once we got on the snowmobiles, we left him in the dust. What do you think is going on back there anyway?"

Jake answered slowly, as he pictured the scene he saw when he turned back and looked at the camp one last time.

"Obviously the man and the boy are stealing. That part isn't hard to figure out. That makeshift tent seemed to be full of their loot. I can't believe how much stolen stuff they had! They must store it there until they can go into town and sell it. Did you see the wallet I was reaching for when Goliath grabbed me? It was a green one with a snowboard on it."

"Not only did I see it, but I was able to grab it while Goliath was focused on throwing you around like a rag doll," Patrick said proudly. "Observe exhibit A," he said, as he carefully pulled it from his pocket. Patrick was holding it on the corner in case the police could identify the man's fingerprints on it later.

"Good work, Detective!" exclaimed Jake. "The hand is quicker than the eye. Of course I was focused on little things like my life, so you could have done just about anything, and I wouldn't have noticed. But I am wondering why you were more concerned about grabbing the wallet, than about helping me. I am your best friend, you know."

"Well I knew you could take care of yourself. Besides, we need some evidence in case they decide to get rid of their loot now that we are on to them."

Jake reached into his backpack for his lunch, but it wasn't there. "Hey, my lunch is gone! I know I put it in there this morning! Is this supposed to be funny?"

"Why would I want your lunch? My mom packed me an incredible submarine sandwich with fruit, and of course, the famous brownies. I have more than enough food for myself. I certainly don't need to steal yours. Could you have forgotten to put it in your back pack? Or maybe Rachel decided to play a trick on you?" Patrick sunk his teeth into his mom's submarine sandwich. It tasted incredibly good. Of course it didn't hurt that he had just run the race of his life, and had burned off all of his breakfast long ago.

"I know for sure that I put my lunch sack in my backpack this morning. And Rachel will sometimes play mean tricks on me, but she would never do something like that."

Patrick hesitated and then handed Jake half of his sandwich. "Thanks, Patrick. I will pay you back someday," Jake said enthusiastically. Without hesitation, Jake took a big bite of the submarine sandwich. "Wow! I'm going to ask your mom to pack my lunches for school. This is the best sandwich I have ever had in my life!"

Suddenly Jake jumped up as he thought of something. "I almost forgot! When we made it back to the snowmobiles I saw a lot of strange footprints. We obviously didn't have time to investigate it, so I didn't say anything at the time. I meant to tell you later. The footprints were about the size of our feet, but I know that we didn't walk around the area that much. I'll bet the mysterious boy stole my lunch! He must have known that we parked there. He seems to always know where we are when we are on the mountain. A bit creepy, really, even though I have to admit that he has come in handy twice now. We really owe him."

"Yes, you are right. We owe him quite a lot. He has saved us from injury twice, and maybe even saved our lives today. I guess you should forgive him for taking your lunch," said Patrick. "At least he didn't get my mom's brownies. Did he take anything else?"

"I don't think so. I didn't have anything else in my bag to take. We had our radios and avalanche equipment in our backpack. That is all that I brought."

"Good. At least you didn't contribute to the pile of loot that they have under the tarp. I would guess that the pile of stolen goods they have is worth thousands of dollars," said Patrick with wide eyes.

"I'm sure you're right. It looks like they have been collecting it for some time. I wonder why they haven't already sold some of it. I'm sure they could use the money for food and clothes," said Jake as he stared up into the sky. *The boy really risked a lot to help us. He risked blowing his cover when he let his dogs save us as we slid down the mountain side. Then he risked his own safety when he stepped in to protect us from the Giant. Why would he do that for two total strangers? Especially since the boy appeared to be a thief. It just doesn't make sense.*

Jake was so lost in his own thought he didn't hear Patrick offer him a brownie. The second time Patrick asked if Jake wanted a brownie, Jake flinched as if he had forgotten Patrick was there. "Oh yeah, sorry, I didn't hear you. Have I ever turned down one of your mom's brownies? I don't think so. I would love one. Thanks."

The boys finished their lunches and rested for a few minutes. It was such a beautiful day they could have stayed in that one spot for hours. The tall pine trees were waving gently in the breeze. The sound of the wind through the trees was very peaceful and relaxing. The white snow was glistening in the sun. The trees still had snow on their branches from last night's snowfall. There were all sorts of animal footprints around this side of the mountain. The boys could see deer prints, fox prints, and even elk prints. Sometimes Jake and Rachel would go hiking up here just to find animal tracks and follow them. Rachel especially was fascinated with animals. She and Jake had even found mountain lion tracks once. They never did see the mountain lion, but Jake couldn't help wondering if it had been watching them that day, maybe even playing games with them. Even though Jake and Rachel had only lived in the mountains for 3 years, they had spent a lot of time up there throughout their entire lives. So they were very comfortable with wildlife. They had grown up knowing what to do in case they ran across a bear, coyote, or mountain lion.

Jake snapped back to reality and asked Patrick, "Why do you think the boy doesn't leave the Giant? He doesn't seem to be like him. The boy seems like a good guy. He also looks very sad and lonely. I saw the Giant push the boy down as we were running away."

"Hey, maybe the boy wants to be saved from the Giant! Maybe that is why he is willing to blow his cover. He wants us to bring the authorities back so he can be rescued from the Giant and not have to steal and be knocked around anymore," said Patrick. "He has to be as scared of the Giant as we are."

"Maybe even more scared if he knows what the Giant is capable of doing," said Jake in a quiet, serious voice.

"Well, let's head down to the base of the mountain before we give the Giant a chance to catch up with us," suggested Patrick.

The boys had an uneventful ride to the parking area. They drove through a lot of trees, so they had to do a lot of switch backs, which took awhile. They had time to think about the mysterious boy and also to enjoy the beautiful scenery. Jake had a vision of the boy sitting on a flat rock, under the beautiful pine trees, enjoying the lunch he took out of Jake's pack. *I just hope he doesn't have to share it with the Giant,* thought Jake as he drove the snowmobile expertly to the parking area.

Chapter 6

"OK, slow down and start from the beginning," said Deputy Jordan. The boys had decided that they needed to report the Giant and the boy to the police because it was obvious that they were in possession of stolen property. Patrick's dad was a Summit County Judge, so the boys knew a little bit about the law. They also knew the Summit County Sheriff department pretty well, mainly because it was a small community and everyone seemed to know everyone. The boys knew that Patrick's dad would be very upset with them, if they did not report their findings to the Sheriff.

The boys told their story in great detail to Deputy Jordan. They told him first about the mysterious trail through the snow, and how obvious it was that someone was dragging things up the mountain. They told him about the boy who came from out of nowhere, and how his dogs saved them from their slide down the mountainside. Then they told him about finding the tent and the large pile of loot that the Giant seemed to have. They also told him that the Giant threatened to hurt Jake, but that Jake escaped his grasp and they were able to get away unharmed. They made sure to mention how the mysterious boy helped them escape from the Giant. "It is funny," said Jake. "The mysterious boy has helped us twice, and both times were at great risk to him. First, he risked giving up his secret location. Then today he risked the anger and violence of the

Giant to help us get a head start. I don't understand why he would want to help two strangers."

"We think that maybe the boy wants us to find them and bring the authorities to rescue him from the Giant," said Patrick.

"Oh, and I almost forgot," said Jake, "one of our friends had his car broken into while he was skiing yesterday. Four wallets were stolen out of his car, and we saw his wallet in the pile of stolen items by the tent."

"We grabbed the wallet in case you need it for evidence," said Patrick, as he held the wallet by the corner and handed it to Deputy Jordan.

"Wow, you boys should be detectives. You have really done your homework on this," said Deputy Jordan, as he let Patrick drop the wallet into a plastic bag. "I wish we could go up there right now and arrest the guy you call "the Giant", but it is late and almost dark. It would be difficult and dangerous to try to find him in the dark. If you can meet me here after school tomorrow, you can show us where they are."

Jake and Patrick looked at each other and nodded. "Sure, we can come by after school tomorrow," said Jake. The boys shook hands with Deputy Jordan and then got in Patrick's truck to drive home.

The boys drove in silence at first, as they both tried to process the events of the weekend. Jake kept thinking about what the mysterious boy had to gain by helping them, and how much the boy had to lose. It just wasn't making sense to him. Why would he risk so much for strangers?

"Well obviously the Giant is the leader, and he is stealing from cars in the parking lots. From the looks of his pile, he has been doing this for a while. But how can they survive in that tent during the winter? It has been pretty cold the last couple of weeks, especially at night," said Patrick.

"Well there are a couple of Summit County organizations that help the homeless. I would bet that if it gets too cold, they go for shelter," said Jake. "There might even be some public buildings that they can get into for protection from the bitter cold. And who knows, maybe they planned to move out of here before we hit the coldest part of the winter."

The boys drove back to Jake's parents' store, to drop off the trailer and snowmobiles. Patrick dropped Jake at his home, and then went to his own home. They both had homework to do and tests to study for. They planned to meet by the school's flag pole, after school Monday.

During the night, a snow storm that was only expected to bring a few inches of snow, decided to hang over Summit County and dump a couple of feet of snow. The boys got up Monday morning to find that school was cancelled. Jake called Deputy Jordan to tell him that they could meet him sooner since school was cancelled.

"I'm sorry Jake, but it is too dangerous," said Deputy Jordan. "The snowstorm is showing no sign of letting up. We can't go up the mountain today. With such a hard snowfall, it would be easy to trigger an avalanche, or even get lost. Call me tomorrow and we will determine whether or not it is safe for us to go up."

Jake and Patrick were frustrated that they could not help Deputy Jordan arrest the Giant today. They felt like the Giant would have a chance to get away if too much time passed before the Deputy found and arrested him. But there wasn't much they could do about the weather. So they decided to make the most of it and snowboard all day. It was too dangerous to snowboard in the backcountry, but they could snowboard inbounds, at a ski resort. It was hard to see, with the snow coming down so hard. But the powder was great, and the boys had so much fun that they were no longer thinking about the Giant and his huge pile of stolen treasures. Every now and then they did wonder how the mysterious boy was staying warm and why he had helped them.

Chapter 7

The next day, Jake and Patrick were both struggling to concentrate on school with so much going on. This was the end of the semester, and it was important for them to do their best on their tests. It wouldn't be long before they started applying to colleges, so their grades were important. Every test counted! Neither one of the boys knew which college they wanted to go to, but they both knew that they were going to college somewhere. Jake wanted to get a degree in business and work in management at one of the Colorado ski resorts. Patrick wanted to get a degree in ministry and work as a youth pastor, as well as coach the Summit County Ski Team. They both knew that they had to do their best in high school if they wanted an opportunity to choose which college they went to.

When the bell rang, the boys met at the flag pole in front of the high school. They jumped in Patrick's truck and rushed to the police station. Deputy Jordan was waiting for them when they arrived.

"Well boys, it has been a couple of days," said Deputy Jordan. "Do you think you can still remember where the Giant and his stolen goods are hiding? We have gotten a lot of snow since then, so we won't be able to use your tracks to help us find the location."

"We can definitely find it," said Patrick confidently. "I have been up there many times, and the two of us have been there twice in the last few days."

"Alright then, let's head out. Deputy Hines will join us. You are going to guide us to an area near the tent, but then you will wait while we approach the tent and arrest the Giant. We can't risk putting you in danger," said Deputy Jordan. "All four of us will wear avalanche beacons, because so much snow has fallen in the last 48 hours. I hope that we don't have to use them, but I know that you boys are trained in avalanche rescue and survival."

The boys and the deputies got their gear together and prepared for their trip up the mountain. The boys began to get nervous. What if the Giant had moved? Or what if they couldn't find the tent because there was so much new snow? They didn't want to waste the deputies' time taking them on a snowmobile ride for no reason.

They took 3 snowmobiles up the mountain. The two deputies were each on their own snowmobile and the boys shared one. The boys tried to repeat what they did on Sunday. They tried to ride up to the east of the tent and go up past where they thought it was. They parked the snowmobiles in a protected area and explained to the officers how to get to the tent from there.

"Deputy Jordan, are you sure that we can't come with you?" asked Jake. "It is hard to describe to you just how to get there from here."

"Jake, I would like to have you lead us there. But, having you there at the time of the arrest, would be putting the two of you in danger," said Deputy Jordan. "We will arrest the Giant and the boy, and hike back up here as soon as possible."

"You are going to arrest the boy?" exclaimed Patrick.

"At this point, we have to arrest the boy if he is there," explained Deputy Jordan. "Back at the police station, we will decide whether or not we release him. It depends on his level of involvement. We also need to determine whether he has family in the area."

The deputies put on their snowshoes and headed in the direction of the tent. Jake and Patrick had their fingers crossed that they were sending the deputies in the right direction. The boys felt useless sitting on the snowmobiles, waiting for the deputies to return with the Giant and the mysterious boy.

After what seemed like an eternity, but what was probably only 30 minutes, the boys heard an explosion. They both looked up in time to see a huge mountain of snow tumbling down from the top of the mountain. Someone had triggered an avalanche with a gunshot and it was headed for the deputies.

Chapter 8

The deputies walked as quickly and quietly as they could in their snowshoes. They were starting to think that they were not on the right path, when suddenly Deputy Jordan said, "I see the tent! Let's turn toward it and approach from this side."

Deputy Hines agreed, so they immediately turned off the trail and headed down to the left side of the camp. As the deputies got closer to the tent, they saw a young boy playing with two dogs on the other side of the campsite. The deputies were still too far away for the boy to have seen or heard them yet.

Suddenly a loud CRACK rang out through the trees. The deputies knew without a doubt that it was the sound of a gun. They stopped suddenly and looked around to see where the shot came from. The boy froze, looked up and locked eyes with Deputy Jordan just as a tidal wave of snow was tumbling down the mountain, wiping out everything in its path. The boy yelled, "WATCH OUT!" as he pointed to the deputies, but it was too late. The deputies looked up just as the wall of snow knocked them off of their feet. As the deputies and the tent were being swept down the mountain, Deputy Jordan thought that he could see an arm of a man in the snow, but quickly forgot about the arm as he tried to remember what to do in an avalanche. The deputies had both been trained on how to survive an avalanche, but they had never had to use their training before. They began to use their arms to swim as if the snow was water, desperately trying to keep their heads above the snow. It was getting harder and harder to keep their heads up as the snow continued down the mountainside. Finally, as the snow sucked him under, Deputy Jordan tried to stick his hand up above the snow, but his arms and legs were pinned and he couldn't move. The only thing he could do was wiggle his head to make a small air pocket so that he did not immediately suffocate in the snow. He only had a short time before he would run out of oxygen, but the air pocket would help a little.

The boys watched in horror as the massive wall of snow thundered down the side of the mountain. Patrick had helped with avalanche rescue before, but neither one of the boys had actually witnessed an avalanche. They had seen avalanches on TV, but that didn't come close to what they were seeing right now.

"OH NO!" Jake and Patrick yelled at once after the avalanche stopped.

"The avalanche had to be close to the deputies and the tent!" exclaimed Jake. "What should we do?!"

"We have no choice!" replied Patrick. "We have to head that way to find them in case they got buried! We don't have much time!"

The boys jumped on the snowmobile and went as fast as they could toward the avalanche, each saying a silent prayer for the safety of the deputies and anyone else who may have been caught in the avalanche. Fear gripped them both. What if the avalanche hit the deputies, the boy and the Giant? Would they have time to find all 4 of them?

Jake and Patrick slowed down when they got close to what used to be the campsite. They saw the mysterious boy and his dogs running down through the clearing that the avalanche had just made. The boys jumped off of the snowmobiles and caught up with the boy.

"Did you see if the avalanche got anyone?" asked Jake breathlessly as they continued to run down the mountain.

"Yes! It hit both of the officers and I think it also got my uncle! I could see them part of the way down, but I lost them right about here."

Jake and Patrick pulled out their avalanche probes and receivers, and got to work without saying a word. They spread out and each of them zigzagged back and forth across the path of the avalanche. The boys always took avalanche equipment with them in the backcountry. Jake had never had to use his, but he had very good training on how to do it. And both of the boys knew that they didn't have much time. Every minute counted!

The dogs seemed to know instinctively that they were looking for buried people. They ran further down the mountain and seemed to be doing their own sweep of the area. The mysterious boy followed the dogs, looking for any signs of the missing people.

Jake felt like it was taking forever to find them and started to panic. He checked his watch and it had already been 10 minutes. They still had some time, but not much. Suddenly Patrick yelled, "Over here! I think I found one of them!" Patrick was carefully probing the snow with his avalanche pole. After 3 or 4 probes he stopped and said "I think I felt something. Pull out your shovel and help me." Jake and Patrick began to dig carefully and they soon found an arm of one of the deputies, but they couldn't tell which one. They uncovered his head and saw that it was Deputy Hines. He was moaning, which meant he was breathing. Patrick finished digging the deputy out, while Jake continued his search for Deputy Jordan.

About 20 feet away Jake saw what looked like a glove in the snow. He ran over and sure enough, his probe indicated that someone was there. He quickly and carefully dug by the glove and found Deputy Jordan who was a bit shaken, but fine. As Deputy Jordan was getting up out of the snow, Jake realized that the mysterious boy was yelling "Uncle! Uncle!" as he ran to where the dogs were digging. Patrick and Jake ran down to help the dogs dig. The boy's uncle wasn't completely buried, so he was breathing. But his head was bleeding and he appeared to be unconscious. He must have hit his head on a rock or tree, as he tumbled in the snow. Deputy Jordan called for help to get the unconscious man down the mountain.

Everything had happened so quickly, that Jake and Patrick had just acted on instinct. But once they realized that everyone was going to be alright, the boys started to think about what had just happened.

"Where did the shot come from that triggered the avalanche?" asked Jake.

"I think the man you call "the Giant" shot his gun into the air to give us a warning," said Deputy Hines. "He wanted to scare us away. But what he didn't realize is that a loud noise like that, combined with the large amount of heavy snow that we got yesterday, would probably create an avalanche."

Flight for Life came in a helicopter and took the Giant to the nearest hospital. The deputies took the Mysterious Boy down to the police station. Jake and Patrick rode their snowmobile down the mountain and headed home for some much needed rest.

Chapter 9

The boys both had a big week at school. They had tests in all of their classes and Jake had two basketball games. Jake and Patrick both work very hard to get good grades in school so that they are allowed to snowboard, snowmobile, and do all of the fun outdoor activities that they enjoy. If they don't keep their grades up, their parents' won't allow them to do anything fun.

Thursday night, Jake and Patrick, as well as several of their friends from school, met at their weekly Fellowship of Christian Athletes (FCA) meeting. They had both been active in FCA since their freshman year of high school. This year Jake was the president of FCA. His counselor, Ms. Atkins, was the adult sponsor of the group. She helped Jake organize monthly speakers as well as the weekly agenda. At the beginning of ninth grade, Patrick didn't like the FCA very much because he didn't know many of the kids who attended. But now he likes it so much that he never misses a meeting. A former NFL player spoke at Tuesday's meeting. His story really motivated the kids to work hard in school, work hard in sports, but still remember to take time for God, church and family.

After the FCA meeting was over, Ms. Atkins walked up to Jake and Patrick. "I read about you guys and your big weekend in the newspaper yesterday," she said. "It sounds like you really did a lot to help the police catch that robber. I'm proud of you two, but I have to point out that you put yourself in danger more than once. You have to be more careful in the future and let the police handle it from the beginning."

"I know, you are right", said Jake. "I had this same conversation with Detective Jordan and then again with my mother and father. We didn't realize that we needed to notify the police until it was already a bit dangerous. But we promise that next time we will be more alert, and notify the police sooner."

Ms Atkins smiled and said, "That's what I want to hear!"

As Jake was walking away, he turned and asked Ms. Atkins if she had read the entire newspaper article. "Yes, I did", she said. "Why?"

"Well I haven't been home today to read it, and I'm wondering if they said what happened to the boy."

"Well it turns out that he ran away from home last summer," Ms. Atkins said. "His name is Daniel, and he lives in El Paso, TX. He hitchhiked to Colorado last summer and has been living with his uncle in the mountains. Obviously, his uncle is going to jail for quite a while, so Daniel can't stay with him. They also said that Daniel missed his parents and wanted to go home, but his uncle wouldn't let him. Daniel's parents had no idea where he went, and they have been worried sick about him. His parents are on their way here to pick him up and drive him back to El Paso. It sounds like he will be pretty excited to see them."

"Not to mention the excitement of sleeping in his own bed!" exclaimed Patrick. "We saw what they were living in, and that tent couldn't have been very warm or comfortable."

As Jake and Patrick were walking out with their friends, they overheard Aaron ask, "Did you hear about all of the hurt animals that have been showing up in town? I read a little about it in the paper, and didn't think much of it at first. But now Ryan said that his dog disappeared for a day and came back limping and with a bloody leg!"

"Wow! I hadn't heard about that! How many animals have been injured?" asked Jake.

"It has been going on for almost 3 weeks, and over a dozen animals have been hurt," explained Aaron. "The owners have no idea where their animals have been, and the police have no leads."

"Hmmmmm," said Patrick, as he smiled at Jake. "It sounds like we have a mystery to solve this weekend."

"Here we go again!" said Jake with a laugh.

Printed in the United States
By Bookmasters